PREY:

WHAT YOU NEED TO KNOW ABOUT THE NEW RELEASED PREY MOVIE

Eva L White

Table of contents

Chapter 1:*Prey movie information*

EARLIER, MAY 16: 20th Century Studios today revealed that its action-thriller Prey, the newest installment in the Predator franchise, will premiere exclusively on Hulu in the United States on August 5th. The film was released as a Star+ Original in Latin America and a Star Original on Disney+ in all other regions.

Prey, a film about a young, strong, and expert fighter named Naru (Amber Midthunder), is set 300 years ago in the Comanche Nation. When danger approaches her camp, she goes out to defend her people since she was reared in the shadow of some of the most renowned hunters that roam the Great Plains. A highly developed extraterrestrial predator with technologically sophisticated armament is the prey she hunts and eventually encounters, leading to a fierce and scary battle between the two foes.

The movie was directed by Dan Trachtenberg (The Boys, 10 Cloverfield Lane) based on a screenplay by Patrick Aison (Jack Ryan). Produced by John Davis (The Predator) and Jhane Myers (Monsters of God), Prey' 20th Century Studios also included executive producers Lawrence Gordon (Watchmen), Marty Ewing (It Chapter Two), James E. Thomas, John C. Thomas, and Marc Toberoff (Fantasy Island). The key to making the movie come to life was giving the Comanche a realistic representation that would resonate with Indigenous peoples. Myers, a renowned director, Sundance fellow, and Comanche nation member, is well-known for her commitment to films about the Comanche and Blackfeet nations and her concern for preserving the Native American cultural heritage. The consequence is that the majority of the cast in the movie is made up of

Native and First Nations actors, such as Midthunder from The Ice Road, Dakota Beavers, Stormee Kipp from Sooyii, Michelle Thrush from The Journey Home, and Julian Black Antelope (Tribal).

Chapter 2:**Summary of prey**

According to its advertising, "Prey" tells the narrative of the firstor other electronic or mechanical methods, without the prior written permission of the publisher, except in the case of brief quotations embodied in critical reviews and certain other Predator extraterrestrials to visit Earth. This one is equipped with slightly vintage versions of the weapons used in the original movie by the late actor Kevin Peter Hall. The Predator operates in the same way, though; it is a hunter and seeks for prized prey. This makes Naru (Amber Midthunder), a teenage warrior who aspires to hunt like the men in her tribe, especially her brother Taabe, a type of kindred spirit for the monster (Dakota Beavers). The males make fun of Naru, saying that hunting is something that only men should do, but we see that she can hold her own in a battle. She is three times more attentive than the others and twice as tough as she appears to be. The first person to discover a new creature on their property is Naru. Maybe it's connected to that fiery streak of fire she earlier saw in the sky.

Taabe hardly tolerates Naru's company as they search for a lion that has been skulking around. In their initial scenes, Midthunder and Beavers almost instantly establish an amicable sibling connection. Once the true threat materializes, their link increases our concerns. Naru finds a snake that has been skinned and some unusual prints. She informs Taabe, "Something scared off the lion," but he is not amused by her assertion that it is a "monster from childhood fantasies." As it advances up the animal food chain, the Predator pulls out the spine of a brazen wolf to teach it a lesson about selling woof tickets. When it mercilessly slaughters the bear that was pursuing Naru and her devoted mud, she finally gets to witness it.

One wonders that "Prey" hadn't given us a decent glimpse of the Predator previously because the sequence with the bear is so well constructed. An explosion of blood reveals the unseen Predator as it yanks the bear from its chase and lifts it up for the kill. When Naru notices this, she flees like the dickens. So follows a string of expertly written pursuit scenes, during which our nemesis eviscerates its victims in both well-known and novel ways. Another reference is made to one of the finest lines from the first movie: "If it bleeds, we can kill it." It does bleed, and at one point Naru uses the bright green blood as battle paint.

A swarm of unkempt French fur
trappers adds another aspect of
danger (as well as new fuel for
viewers hungry for Predator-based
slaughter). When Naru discovers a
field of skinned buffalo, she prays
over them because she believes the
monster is responsible for creating
them. She soon understands that man,
that other horrible predator, is to
blame. The trappers are much more
evil than the Predator, despite the fact
that they concur with Naru that there
is something supernatural out there.
So when they begin to be splattered,
we are not sad.

Even if there are no "choppas" for anybody to reach in 1719, "Prey" is a respectable replacement for Ah-original. nuld's Naru is deserving of being included on the list of resilient characters that can stand up to the Predator. She handles all of her enemies with equal parts intelligence and brute force, eliminating them with gruesome efficiency. Even though nature might be a brutal foe, she is prepared for it. They are the protagonists of the plot, and their town hums with a sense of kinship, thus the movie paints a portrayal of her Comanche country without otherizing them. The movie is primarily in English, but it doesn't threaten our ability to suspend disbelief (a complete Comanche language version was supposedly also shot concurrently).

Fans of "Predator" won't be let down by "Prey," despite the usual cry from immature guys who haven't even watched the film but are already dismissing it as "too woke." It's a thrilling, entertaining, and unexpectedly touching emotional amusement park experience. I couldn't help but smile as Naru finally let out the battle cry she had been denied before. It's too bad I couldn't do it in front of a crowd of enthusiastic spectators.

Chapter 3: **CAST**

AMBER MIDTHUNDER	**NARU**
DANE DI LIEGRO	**PREDATOR**
DAKOTA BEAVERS	*TAABE*
STEFANY MATHIAS	*SUMU(CHIEF WIFE)*
STORMEE KIPP	*WASAPE*
MICHELLE THRUSH	*ARUKA*

JULIAN BLACK ANTELOPE	CHIEF KEHETU
BENNETT TAYLOR	RAPHAEL
MIKE PATERSON	BIG BEARD
TYMON CARTER	HUUPI
NELSON LEIS	WAXED MUSTACHE
SKYE PELLETIER	TABU
DIONICIO VIRVER	NATIVE COMANCHE WARRIOR
GERONIMO	COMANCHE

Chapter 4: **5 FACTS TO KNOW ABOUT PREY**

Here are five facts concerning Prey that you should be aware of:

1. *It's a story that goes back to the basics and nods to the original*

The Predator has appeared in comic books, video games, and the first six films in the franchise. Which brings up two inquiries: Why produce a Predator sequel? And why was the 18th century chosen for the story?

According to Trachtenberg, "I believe the thing that made everyone say yes to it so fast was that it seemed like, on one hand, it was harkcning back to the original." Back to the basics, I say. It plays all the same notes that the original film did while simultaneously seeming completely new and different.

The Prey tale has to rely on a concept that would already make a fantastic movie, according to the director. "It doesn't seem separate when the franchise and the IP are included. It seems as though both movies have improved. And as a result, that was a major component of the movie's pitch.

2. *The movie places the highest priority on indigenous representation*

According to Jhane Myers, this is the first movie that has ever been made entirely in our language. And this is the first brand-new, straight-out-of-the-box movie to employ a local tongue.

According to Trachtenberg, in addition to the English-Comanche hybrid that will be made accessible on Hulu and that will be seen by the majority of viewers, a separate Comanche cut will also be made available.

A previous version of the film, he continued, "was completely in Comanche and then it switches, functioning a little more like The Hunt for Red October." Unfortunately, some earlier viewers found the movie to be quite confused due to the variety of terminology used.

Because of Myers' strong leadership, the entire ensemble came back to speak their roles in Comanche to guarantee the authenticity came through.

3.A BRAVE ACTION HERO, AMBER MIDTHUNDER

When Amber Midthunder portrayed Kerry Loudermilk on FX's ground-breaking comic book series Legion, she had her first opportunity to display her combat prowess. She has since increased both her on-screen and behind-the-scenes fighting experience.

She and the rest of the actors went to a four-week boot camp where they trained with weapons and worked closely with the stunt team to be ready for this production. But preparation can only go so far, and as Midthunder noted, the shoot was fraught with difficulties.

There's just no way to prepare for experiencing all that went into creating this movie, she continued. "There were rivers, mud pits, monsters, and a lot of other things, like ash, smoke, and things like that. You can't really prepare for the wide variety of experiences that so many characters have.

The biggest detail Amber might not have anticipated is the action hero status she obtains with this performance. Even though the actress is modest, she acknowledges the honor and accepts the responsibilities that goes along with it.

No matter who played Naru, this movie would have been made, according to Midthunder. None of it was lost on me when I was picked to accomplish that. It's a major issue for the franchise as well as for women in general and Indigenous women in particular. There is no hero among us. In movies, TV shows, or other forms of media, we don't have anybody to look up to who we can be proud of or who can symbolize all we want to see or mimic. So, to have a character like this in a movie? It is absolutely everything to me.

4. *This predator is more ferocious and uses primitive technology.*

The Predator in Prey has a somewhat different appearance from the extraterrestrial invaders we're used to seeing since the tale it's portraying takes place three millennia in the past. Additionally, the technology of his weaponry is more basic.

According to Trachtenberg, "He doesn't have the same technology as he did in some earlier incarnations we have seen previously." In numerous instances, he is equipped with whole new weapons that seem more archetypal than some of the other things we've seen.

According to Trachtenberg, the idea of time is frequently absent in the science fiction and fantasy genres when it comes to technological advancement. That trap doesn't catch prey.

"Despite the fact that so much time has passed between the films, the games, and all of those other things, it's not like you've ever seen technology develop in any of the Star Wars movies. Star Trek, Lord of the

Rings, and other films give the impression that technology has stood still. Making it seem a little early than what we had observed gave me the impression that I was making significant progress. Of course, in actual terms, 300 years would have been far more dramatic. But I believe that this makes sense in cinematic logic.

5. *More Predator movies might be on the horizon.*

It's safe to say that moviegoers weren't at all ready for a Predator prequel to come out in 2022, much less one that diverges from the established canon's expected parameters and timeframe.

Prey is finished and available for viewing, therefore it begs the question of whether the franchise will continue to feature original tales in the future. That's a query with a large maybe for an answer.

Chapter 5:**Predator movies**

Franchises frequently begin with nobody with a great idea. In reality, Predator was created by two unknowns, brothers Jim and John Thomas, who were struggling screenwriters and imagined what it would be likc if an alien-vs.-Rocky sequel were to be filmed. The story, which was originally titled Hunter, made its way to super-producer Joel Silver, who was seeking for their next project after collaborating with Arnold Schwarzenegger on Commando. At this time,

Schwarzenegger was just starting to get popular. His films were considered garbage, but as each one gained popularity, they continued growing a little bit more... Well, maybe not ambitious, but at least a little bit more expansive.

As a result, Arnold and his commando friends battle a huge, hideous, amazing extraterrestrial designed by the Stan Winston studio, complete with mandibles, long hair, and the power to vanish. Put that man up against Arnold, and you have a winner. Predator received mixed reviews from critics, despite Roger Ebert's support, but it was a huge hit with viewers. Arnold grew in size, the screenwriters produced Wild Wild West, and a franchise was established.

It took 15 years for the subsequent generation of filmmakers, who had all grown up watching Predator on VHS, to revive the series after a disastrous sequel.Below are ratings of the seven Predator films in light of this week's release of Prey, the first prequel in the series. Yes, even the ones that contain the Alien from Alien.

7. *Requiem in Alien vs. Predator (2007)*

Hollywood today is very much about protecting the brand and making sure the movie isn't so horrible that it kills

the series. The Alien vs. Predator
franchise, of which it was the first
and last sequel, was destroyed by
Alien vs. Predator: Requiem, and the
other two were so severely wounded
that they would both have to start
again in the next four years. Requiem,
which was directed by the founders of
the special effects studio Hydraulx,
has the look and feel of a movie that
was simply hired by the special
effects people to direct in order to
keep the cost of the computer
graphics as low as possible. Although
you can (sometimes) make out their
faces in the dark, the human
characters—who, regrettably, make
up a considerably larger portion of
game than the title characters—are

not special effects. It's easy to see the representatives for Predator and Alien begging to have their names removed from this film.

6.*Predator 2 (1990)*

A complex narrative involving drug traffickers, a heat wave in Los Angeles, and internal LAPD politics takes the place of the original movie's simplicity, which had humanity stuck in the forest with a space invader killing them one by one. What happened to just allowing Predator to go on the hunt? Predator 2 isn't entirely terrible, in part because the Predator concept is expanded, eventually leading to the addition of several Predators. They are only hunters, just like us; they are not monsters. The film is nasty, but not necessarily dumb, pseudo-RoboCop ugliness from the late 1980s, and it was a massive disappointment that ended the franchise for decades. Even so, the outtake in which Danny Glover dances with many Predators could make it all worthwhile.

5. The predator (2018)

This most recent remake sought to adopt a slightly irreverent tone while embracing the hard-R spirit of the original movie and recognizing how out of date it was. Unfortunately,

Shane Black, who portrayed one of Schwarzenegger's buddies in the 1987 movie, acts as co-writer and director of this adaptation of The Predator. The Black Touch wasn't really helpful, though: Even the director of the films Kiss Kiss Bang Bang and The Nice Guys, which expertly balanced humor, action, and character, was powerless to stop this franchise. Boyd Holbrook, Trevante Rhodes, Keegan-Michael Key, and Olivia Munn make for an appropriately endearing ragtag group that faces off against the Predator, but the movie lacked the inspired mayhem of director Shane Black's best work, trying so hard to recreate the anything-goes mentality of '80s movies that it never feels like anything other than pastiche. Simply said, The Predator plays like the kind of dreadful franchise reboot that the characters in a Shane Black script would mock.

4.Alien vs predator (2004)

Reverse history: When James Cameron realized Fox had opted to produce an Alien vs. Predator movie rather than a fifth Alien movie, he was in the middle of writing the story for that movie. After declaring that the new movie would "destroy the franchise's authenticity" and that it "was Frankenstein Meets Werewolf, Universal basically grabbing their assets and trying to play them off against one other," Cameron immediately stopped writing. (Cameron nailed the next 20 years of popular culture virtually on the head.) It didn't wind up being the end of the world or the Alien franchise, for that matter, and the movie itself isn't really all that bad. It turned out to be a great idea to base the movie on a comic book rather than the films that came before it, since this prevented Alien vs. Predator from becoming a McTiernan or Cameron rip-off and allowed it to just be huge stupid fun. Sanaa Lathan had an astonishingly (and excessively) passionate and dedicated lead performance in this dopey, entertaining film, which was directed by Paul W.S. Anderson in usual, brilliantly trashy way.

3. *Predator (2010)*

Robert Rodriguez had grown up adoring Predator and was only just beginning out, after El Mariachi and Desperado but before Spy Kids. He had created a script that dealt with a number of experienced murderers being dumped on a foreign world where they are pursued by predators, as if Predator 2 had never taken place. It was 15 years before Fox execs notified Rodriguez they wanted to film the script: They relaunched the series with some changes and Hungarian director Nimrod Antal at the helm, along with an impressive cast that included Laurence Fishburne, Alice Braga, Walton Goggins, Danny Trejo, Topher Grace, a then-unknown Mahershala Ali, and an obscenely bulked-up Adrien Brody, if you can imagine such a thing. Predators isn't flawless—it basically unravels by the end—but it's creative and imaginative, and it was a trailblazer in its attempt to restart a brand by doing something entirely new. It is a B-movie that is both aware of and proud of its status as such.

2. Prey(2022)

Prey is a sincere attempt to change up the formula, much like Predators. (For one thing, the movie's name doesn't even mention the Predator.) Director Dan Trachtenberg expands a property by keeping things quite straightforward, as he did with 10 Cloverfield Lane. Back in the early 18th century, an ambitious Comanche warrior named Naru (Amber Midthunder) is tasked with protecting her tribe from the terrifying alien. Prey can be compared to The New World with a lot more bloodshed and frightening alien sightings, which is oversimplifying but not totally incorrect. (The locations in Canada are quite breathtaking.) Thankfully, the crude prejudices that would have been pervasive in the 1987 original did not appear in Trachtenberg's portrayal of Indigenous North Americans, and the movie even slips in some admirable reflections about colonialism. But what makes Prey so satisfying is its persistent capacity to provide frightening action moments. In addition, Naru is the franchise's most intriguing lead character since Dutch said, "If it bleeds, we can murder it." Prey is the first Predator film in a very long time that isn't overtly horrible, and yet, even if we wish we could have watched it on the big screen instead of Hulu, we fear people will overrate it.

1.Predator (1987)

It began as a rescue operation but turned into a bloody battle with an unknown extraterrestrial warrior. Few movies are more blatantly 80s than the original Predator, which starred rising star Arnold Schwarzenegger in the role of Dutch, the commander of a top-secret team of elite commandos who travels to Central America only to encounter an intergalactic killing machine. Predator, which blends shoot-'em-up extravaganza with a clever narrative hook, is a hybrid of Rambo and Aliens, displaying the type of beautiful Reagan-era excess typical of its blockbuster period. Additionally, Arnold found a top-tier action director in John McTiernan who was just beginning to make his mark. (The release of The Hunt for Red October and Die Hard was imminent.) What might be less recalled is how fascinating it is to witness Schwarzenegger, for once, take on someone of his own size — bigger, actually. You already know by heart the famous memes and quotable speech. In all honesty, one of Predator's scariest scenes is when Arnold is effortlessly lifted up by the alien as his helpless feet are dangling over the ground. Dutch virtually needs to turn into a feral beast to fight the Predator once Carl Weathers, Bill Duke, Jesse Ventura, and the rest of his group are gone; this change brings out a wildness and unexpected fragility in that decade's most hyped action hero. Predator was high-concept and throwaway, yet thanks to its wild excitement, it has managed to endure. It was cheesy, gruesome, kind of silly, and somehow endearing.